CONTENTS

This edition published in 1992 by NDM Publications, Inc.
NDM Publications, Inc
30 Inwood Road
Rocky Hill, CT 06067

Produced by Twin Books Ltd
Kimbolton House
117A Fulham Road
London SW3 6RL

Copyright © 1991 Twin Books UK Ltd

Directed by HELENA Productions Ltd.
Illustrated by Van Good-Lefevre-Loiseaux

ISBN 1-56657-022-0

Printed in Hong Kong

The Ugly Duckling

GREAT POND PUBLISHING

One warm spring morning, after Mother Duck had been sitting on her nest of eggs for some weeks, she heard a *tap! tap! tap!* Soon her ducklings pecked and scratched their way out of the eggs. They looked about and blinked their big eyes at the bright light.

"Welcome to the world," said Mother Duck gently. "I am your mother!"

The little yellow ducklings quacked excitedly to each other in their tiny voices. The last duckling was still struggling out of his shell. He emerged, much larger than the others, craned his long neck and gave a loud honk.

"Goodness!" exclaimed Mother Duck. The smaller ducklings looked at each other with surprise. The last duckling was gray and gawky. A bit of shell still clung to the top of his head. The long silence was broken by a shrill giggle from one of the ducklings.

Soon they were all laughing and
pointing unkindly at the ugly duckling.

5

The other barnyard fowl came to see what all the laughter was about. They, too, stared at the ugly duckling. Then the rooster crowed his disapproval.

The other ducks jeered. "You're a disgrace to us ducks!" one of them said.

The ugly duckling huddled under his mother's wing. "You should be ashamed of yourselves," quacked his mother angrily, "picking on a helpless little duckling. Leave him alone!"

But the commotion only got worse, as
the turkey and other ducks and chickens
joined the squabble. "He's got to go!"
they honked and clucked and quacked.
Not even the ugly duckling's mother
could protect him.

The ugly duckling found an opening in the wall and fled across the meadow. The loud birds followed him a short distance. Then he could hear their angry voices as he darted under the fence and stumbled into the forest.

The ugly duckling was afraid. Was it his fault that he didn't look like the others? Before long he noticed that the forest was growing darker and colder. "I'll just have to take care of myself," he said. He made a grassy nest under a big tree, and passed his first long night alone, trying not to think of his mother's soft feathers and kind eyes.

The ugly duckling awoke shivering with the cold. He felt lonely and hungry and not at all brave. He began to cry.

Suddenly, he heard voices. A couple of field mice had come to see who was sobbing.

"Hi, there," said the bigger mouse. "I'm Tim and this here's Tom. We want to know what a little thing like you is doing out here by yourself."

As the duckling told his sad story, Tom wrapped his scarf around the duckling's neck to keep him warm.

"Maybe you could be friends with that fella over there," suggested Tom, pointing to a heron in a nearby pond.

"I'll give it a try," responded the ugly duckling doubtfully. He waddled to the water's edge.

The heron greeted the ugly duckling with an unfriendly glare, then hopped up on the bank. His legs were so long that he loomed over the duckling, who turned and fled.

"What you need," said Tim, "is to be with your own kind." He and Tom urged the duckling toward the ducks in a nearby pond.

But when the duckling approached the strange ducks, he was not greeted warmly. The ducklings jeered at him, and the big duck splashed him, quacking, "Go away!"

Crestfallen, the ugly duckling paddled
back to the shore. "No one likes me
because I'm so ugly," he said sadly.
"There now," comforted Tim. "I've
already got a solution to your problem."
He winked at Tom and pointed to a little
farmhouse in a clearing.

The mice urged the duckling to the farmhouse door, promising a warm, dry place to sleep and lots to eat.

Sure enough, when the farmer's wife came out to milk the cow . . .

. . . she scooped up the ugly duckling. "Are you lost?" she asked gently, and brought him into the house.

The duckling slept in a basket that night and had scraps of bread to eat in the morning. But as the days and weeks passed, he felt more and more uneasy in the small house. He longed to swim on the water and feel the breeze ruffle his feathers. He missed his friends the mice, who sometimes came to peek at him through the window.

One day, when the farmer's wife opened the door, the duckling rushed out. "Let's go!" he quacked, and the three friends ran across the meadow.

They played tag on the lakeshore, but the duckling had an unfair advantage because he could swim. That night the duckling found a bush to sleep under, and the mice slept in their burrows.

And so the days of summer passed. The duckling stopped wishing for his own kind, feeling happy by himself or with the mice. Soon it was autumn, and the lake echoed with gunshots as hunting season opened. Many geese and ducks were shot, but the ugly duckling escaped by hiding with the mice.

The birds began flying south, and once the ugly duckling felt a strange longing when he saw three beautiful white birds pass silently overhead.

Winter came as suddenly as the snow one night, and in the morning laughter rang through the air as the ugly duckling and the mice slid down a hill, and shook snow off the trees on to each other. The woods and the meadow looked beautiful cloaked in white, but winter was not so much fun later that day, when it turned bitterly cold.

The three friends decided they had to
seek warmth to survive. The wind blew
at them as they trudged through the snow.

Suddenly Tim shouted, "Look! The farmhouse!" But just
at that moment the duckling collapsed in the snow, and the
mice couldn't rouse him.

"We've got to get help fast," said Tom, "before he freezes.
Quick, run and get the barn mice."

Tim scrambled to the barn, and before long he returned
with helpers.

The mice heaved and pulled and pushed the duckling through the snow, until at last they managed to get him into the barn.

"Over here!" squeaked one of the barn mice. "That's it! Easy does it!"

Tim and Tom were afraid that their friend might never awaken. Lovingly, they made him a nest of straw, and huddled close to him through the long night, patting his feathers with their little paws.

Light slowly filtered into the barn as
morning came, and suddenly the duckling
raised his head. "Where am I?" he asked.
Cheers filled the barn as the mice
shouted with joy.

The duckling listened intently as the mice explained what had happened. "You're the best friends a duck could have," he said to Tim and Tom. "And thanks," he added to the barn mice.

The friends decided to spend the rest of the winter in the barn. They passed the days playing charades and hide-and-seek.

When spring came the duckling yearned again for the woods and the lake. Tim and Tom thought of their snug burrows near the lakeshore.

One day they decided to
return to the lake. They
thanked the barn mice for
their help and friendship
and set off across the
meadow, waving goodbye.

35

When the friends slipped under the fence at the edge of the farm, the ugly duckling suddenly began to cry.

"What is it?" asked Tom. The duckling had remembered the birds he had seen flying south in the fall. They were graceful and white, and all winter their beauty had haunted him. When he told the mice, they tried to cheer him up. "Those were swans you saw," said Tim. "They should be back any day now. I'm sure they'll want you to join them."

But the ugly duckling felt sure that no bird as beautiful and proud as the swans would welcome him, and he only felt worse.

Just then they heard a honking overhead, and looked up to see the swans circling over the lake. The beautiful creatures alighted on the water.

"Come over here!" cried Tom to the duckling. "I've got something to show you."

The duckling joined the mice at the water's edge. At their insistence, he peered at his reflection, and suddenly caught his breath.

The reflection he saw was not that of an ugly duckling at all, but that of a swan! Suddenly, he realized why he had never fit in with the ducks: he had been born a swan. He hardly noticed that the mice had climbed aboard his back. Quickly, he paddled out to greet the swans, his heart pounding.

The other swans stared with surprise when he approached, and the ugly duckling prepared himself for their jeering. As they stretched their long necks toward him, he expected the worst, but instead, they stroked his feathers with their bills, accepting him as one of their own. No one was happier at that moment than the duckling's devoted friends – except, perhaps, the once ugly duckling himself, who had turned into the most beautiful swan of all.

Jack and the Beanstalk

Jack and his widowed mother lived together in a small cottage in the forest. They had a spotted cow that gave rich milk – more than they could drink. So they made cheese and butter from the extra milk to sell at the market.

But one morning the cow went dry. There was no milk to drink and no food to sell. When Jack saw how worried his mother was, he stopped playing with his pet squirrel, Phil, and said: "It's all right, Mother. I'll take the cow to market and sell her. Then we'll have money to live on."

"We'll be back soon, Mother," called Jack, as he led the cow out of the yard. "We're sure to get a good price for our cow, so we won't go hungry."

Two birds had overheard him, and suddenly one of them called out, "We know where you can sell your cow!" Jack loved adventures, so he followed the birds into the forest.

The path showed by the birds led the little group to an old man leaning on a staff deep in the woods.

"So you want to sell that fine-looking cow, do you?" the old man asked, as one of the birds perched on his hat. "I'll take her gladly, in exchange for these magic beans." He showed Jack a handful of beans.

Jack was tempted by the word "magic". He handed over the cow's halter and ran home with the beans.

"Mother, look!" Jack cried, rushing into the cottage.

"What?" exclaimed his mother. "Have you sold the cow already?"

"Yes!" he said excitedly. "In exchange for these magic beans!"

But Jack's mother was very upset when she found he had gotten no money for the cow. "What will we live on?" she said angrily. "These are worthless!" and she threw the beans into the yard.

48

Jack and his mother went to bed sadly that night, after eating the last of their food.

But imagine Jack's surprise when one of the birds he had met the day before awakened him early in the morning. The bird showed him a vine so large that its leaves were bursting through his window! The magic beans his mother had thrown away had grown into an enormous beanstalk overnight!

Jack ran outside. The beanstalk reached so high above the cottage that it disappeared into the clouds. Eagerly, Jack began to climb. "Where do you think we'll end up, Phil?" he asked. But Phil could only wonder, too.

The friends climbed higher
and higher, until they reached a
land above the clouds. In the
distance they saw a great castle.

"Lets find out who lives there," said Jack. "Maybe they'll give us something to eat!" All these adventures were making him hungry.

Jack and his friends made their way to the huge door of the castle. "Is anyone home?" shouted Jack. To his astonishment, a giantess came to the door and stared down at him.

"You're just the boy I need to help with the housework!" she said. "But come in quickly and hide, before my husband comes home, or he'll eat you up."

Jack's hunger overcame his fear, so he ran inside and hid under the dining room table. Then the giant's heavy footsteps shook the castle. Stamping into the room, he roared:

"Fee, fi, fo, fum,
I smell the blood of an Englishman;
Be he alive or be he dead
I'll grind his bones to make my bread!"

Jack shook with fright, but the giantess said to her husband: "You don't smell anything but the nice ox I've cooked for your dinner. Sit down and eat it while it's hot."

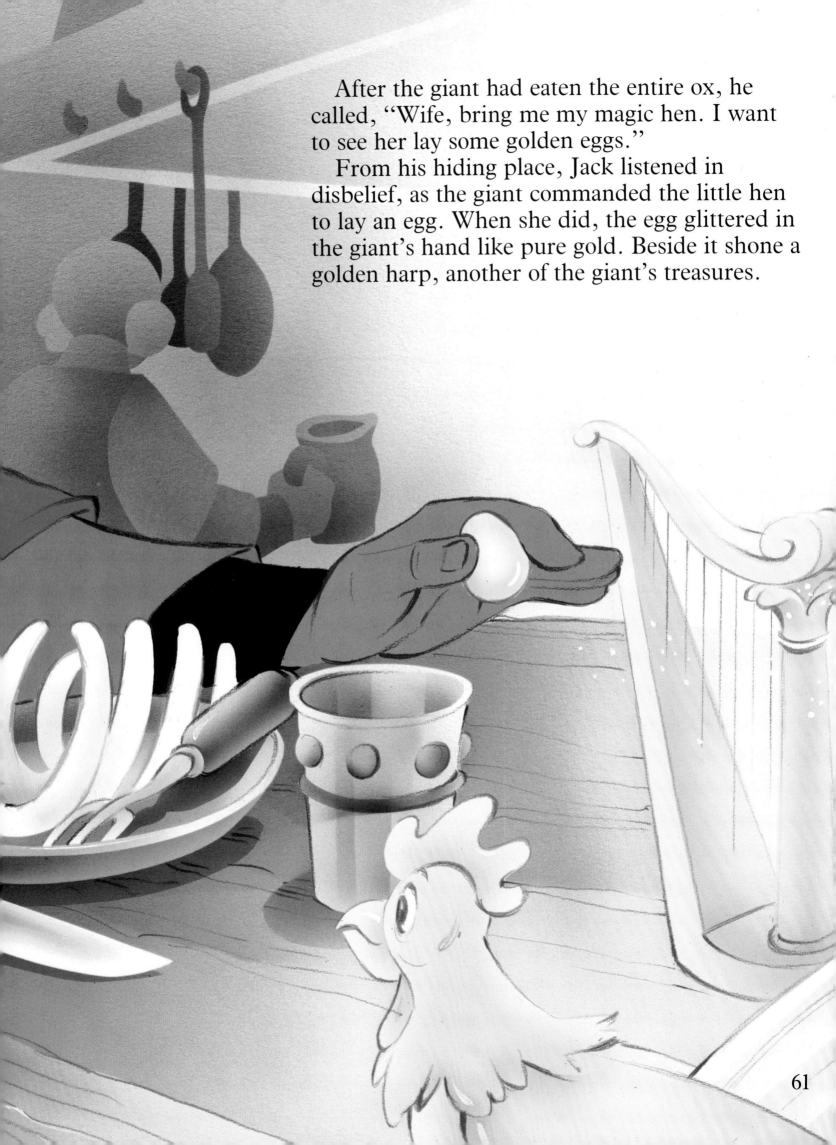

After the giant had eaten the entire ox, he called, "Wife, bring me my magic hen. I want to see her lay some golden eggs."

From his hiding place, Jack listened in disbelief, as the giant commanded the little hen to lay an egg. When she did, the egg glittered in the giant's hand like pure gold. Beside it shone a golden harp, another of the giant's treasures.

When the giant fell asleep at
the table, Jack sprang out of
hiding and seized the magic
hen. With his heart hammering,
he sped toward the window with
the hen tucked under his arm.

The hen clucked with alarm when Jack and Phil leaped out the window. They raced across the plain toward the beanstalk.

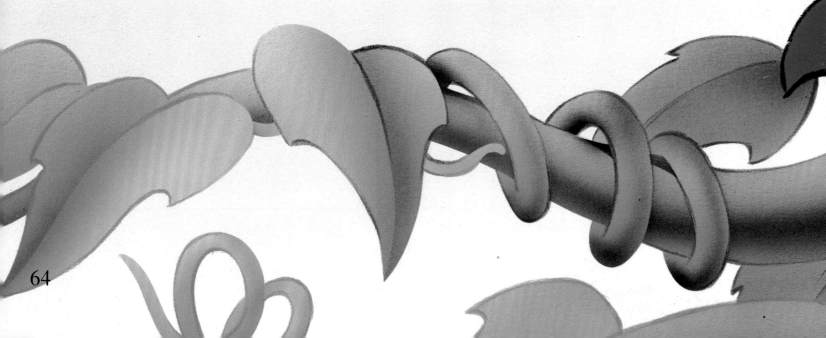

When the hen saw how far it was to the
ground, she squawked so loudly that Phil tried
to hush her. He was afraid she would awaken
the giant.

65

It was too late! The hen's outcry had already aroused the monster. His heavy tread shook the ground like an earthquake as he pursued them!

"That club of his could fell a tree!" cried Jack, as he and Phil scrambled down the beanstalk as fast as they could.

Jack's mother was so happy to see him back safe that she burst into tears. Then Jack showed her the magic hen and told her about the golden eggs.

"We need never be poor again, Mother," he said proudly. The little household was filled with rejoicing.

But Jack was too adventurous to stay quietly at home for long. He kept thinking of the giant's golden harp. One bright morning, he climbed the beanstalk again.

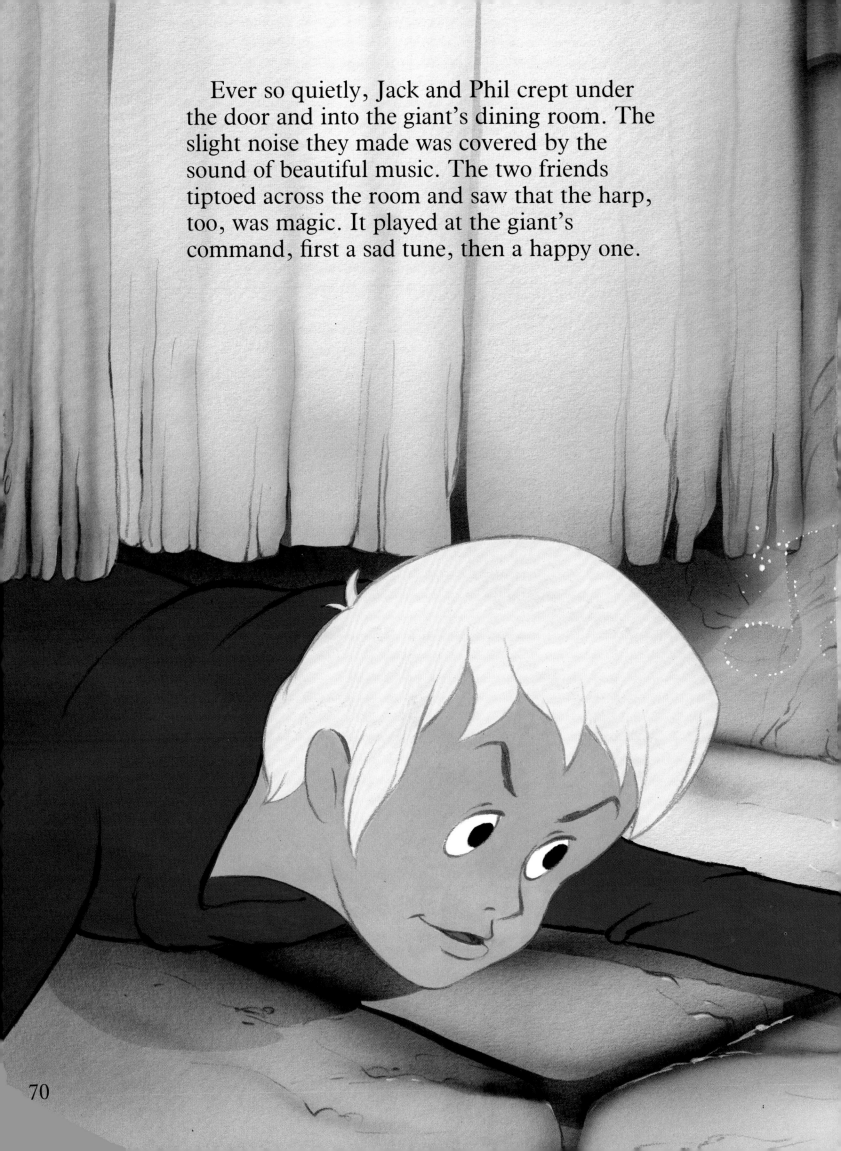

Ever so quietly, Jack and Phil crept under the door and into the giant's dining room. The slight noise they made was covered by the sound of beautiful music. The two friends tiptoed across the room and saw that the harp, too, was magic. It played at the giant's command, first a sad tune, then a happy one.

"Play again!" the giant ordered, and the harp responded with another burst of sweet music that filled the castle. Jack and Phil forgot about caution as they drew closer to listen. Suddenly, the giant spotted them!

"You stole my magic hen!" he roared, seizing his huge club. Jack snatched the harp and ran for his life, with Phil close behind.

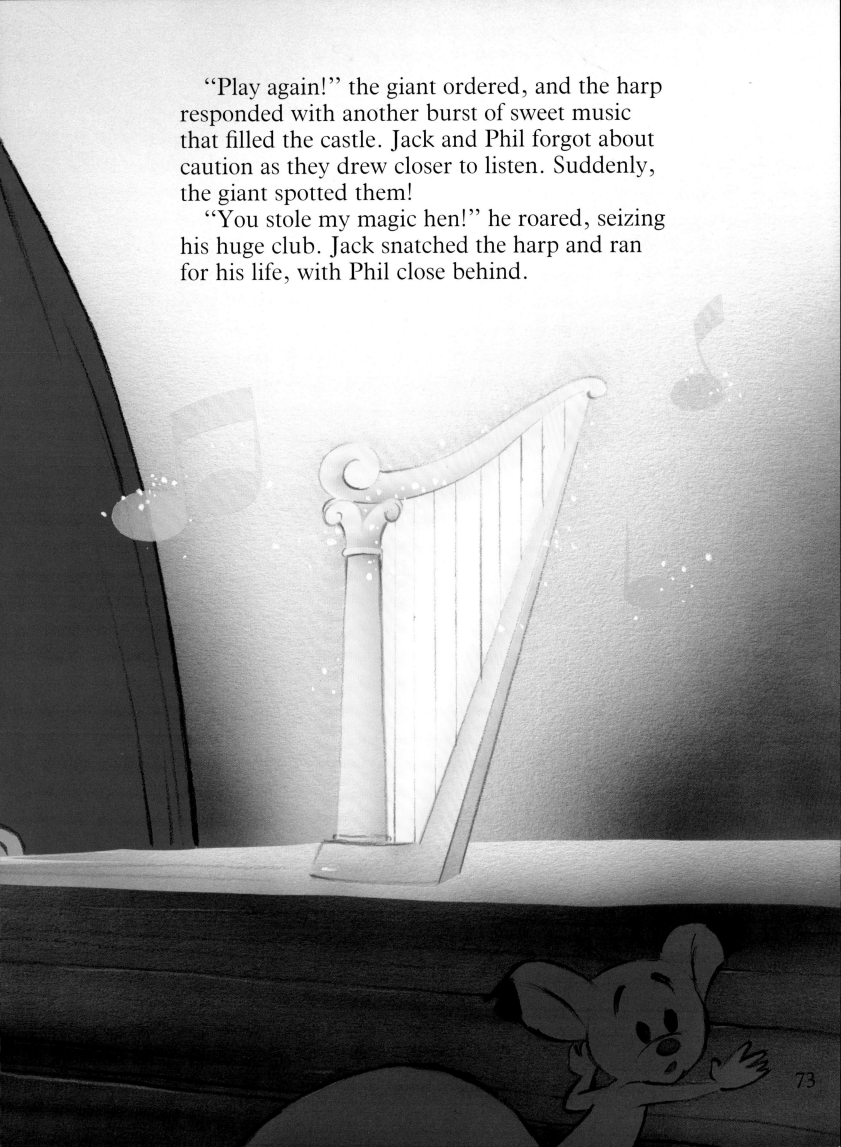

73

"Hurry!" cried their guide. "He's gaining on you!"

Jack and Phil reached the beanstalk and began to climb down. The magic harp was crying, "Master, master!" as the giant followed close behind them.

Luckily, their small size and weight made Jack and Phil much faster than the clumsy giant. They soon reached the ground, and Jack seized an axe and struck at the base of the beanstalk. He chopped with all his strength.

Just as it seemed the giant would catch up with them, the great beanstalk began to sway back and forth. Then, with a loud *crack*, crashed to the ground. The giant fell with it and lay motionless.

"Look, Mother!" cried Jack. "The giant will never frighten anyone again. And we've got his magic harp as well as the hen!"

With that, the faithful bird who had guided Jack through his adventures took flight, and Jack and his mother went into the cottage.

"What a brave, clever boy you are!" said Jack's mother, giving him a hug. "And how glad I am now that you went adventuring." And just as they should, they lived happily ever after.

Little Red Riding Hood

Many years ago there lived, in a cottage by the forest, a mother and her little girl. Since she always wore a red cape and hood, the little girl was called Little Red Riding Hood. She was a pleasant girl, as fond of her grandmother as she was of spending time outdoors with her animal friends.

One day in springtime, Little Red Riding Hood's grandmother became ill, and so the mother made her a pie. Little Red Riding Hood's mother hummed as she rolled the dough and cut the apples, and soon the pie was ready.

The mother carefully packed the pie into a basket for Grandmother, who lived in a cottage at the other side of the woods.

"Bring this to Grandmother. It will make her feel better," said Little Red Riding Hood's mother, handing her the basket. "And she will be happy to see you. Keep to the path, my dear, so you won't get lost. And don't talk to strangers. Tell Grandmother I'll visit her tomorrow."

Little Red Riding Hood was pleased to be entrusted with such an important task. She waved to her mother as she set off on her way. The sun shone brightly, and it seemed that even the flowers waved as they moved in the warm spring breeze. As she walked deeper into the forest, the trees' branches overhead blocked out much of the sunlight. "The path is like a delightful cave!" thought the girl, and she began to skip.

Because Little Red Riding Hood was so kind and gentle, the forest animals liked her. Before long the girl noticed that her animal friends were coming with her. The birds flitted from tree to bush, and the squirrels raced along the branches. Perhaps they thought she was too little to make such a long journey alone.

"It's a lovely day for a trip through the woods," said Little Red Riding Hood, and in a language that only the girl could understand, the animals agreed.

"What is that sound?" Little Red Riding Hood asked herself. She could hear heavy footsteps. Suddenly, a wolf appeared.

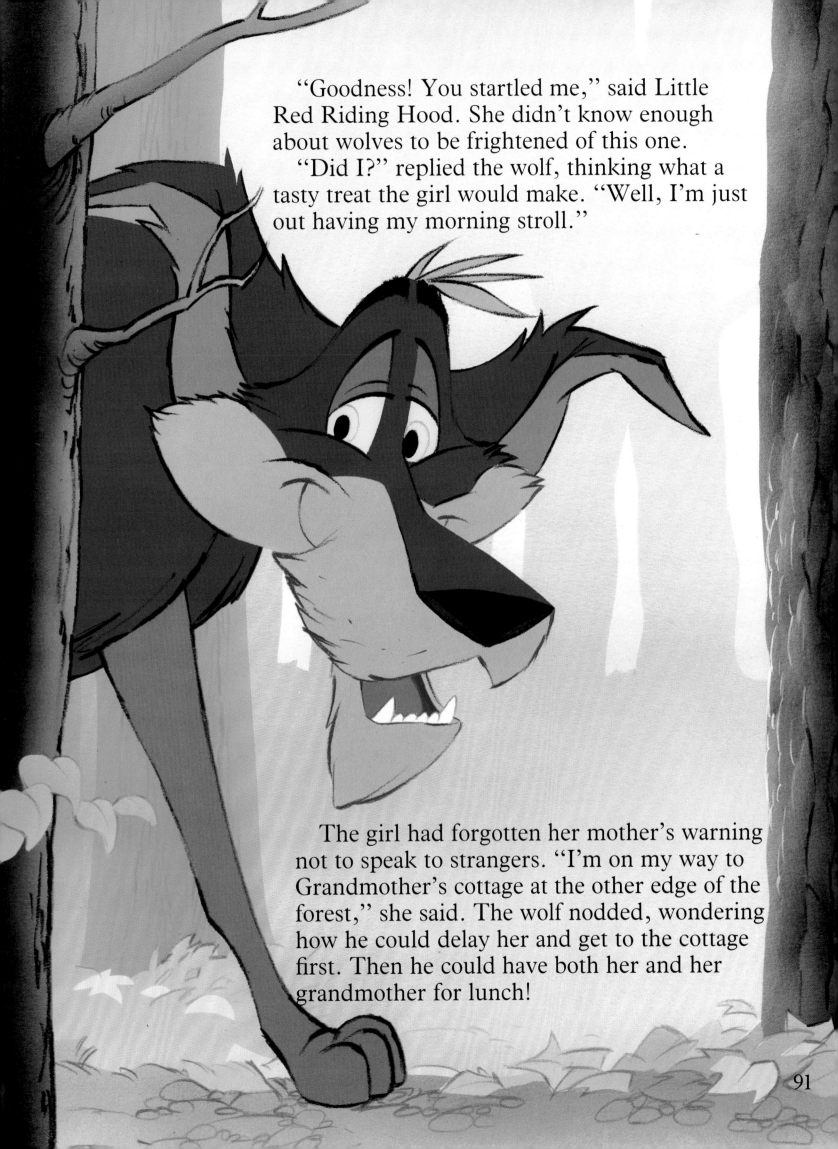

"Goodness! You startled me," said Little Red Riding Hood. She didn't know enough about wolves to be frightened of this one.

"Did I?" replied the wolf, thinking what a tasty treat the girl would make. "Well, I'm just out having my morning stroll."

The girl had forgotten her mother's warning not to speak to strangers. "I'm on my way to Grandmother's cottage at the other edge of the forest," she said. The wolf nodded, wondering how he could delay her and get to the cottage first. Then he could have both her and her grandmother for lunch!

Suddenly, the crafty wolf had an idea. "I think a bouquet of wildflowers would cheer the old lady," he said brightly.

"What a grand idea!" replied Little Red Riding Hood. "I will pick her some flowers right away. How happy she'll be!"

"I'll be on my way now," said the wolf. "I'm sure we'll meet again."

"I hope so!" said the girl. The wolf sauntered into the woods, but as soon as he was out of sight . . .

. . . he dashed away, running as fast as he could toward Grandmother's cottage. "This is my lucky day," he thought. "Not one, but *two* meals for my hungry tummy." He knew just where the cottage was, so he wasted no time heading toward it, leaping over logs and dodging trees.

Little Red Riding Hood ran to find her animal friends. "Guess what?" she asked them. "I met the nicest fellow, and he suggested I bring Granny a bouquet. Now isn't that a fine idea?'

"I know where the prettiest flowers are!" exclaimed one of the squirrels, pointing into the woods.

Little Red Riding Hood had also forgotten her mother's warning not to stray off the path! She and the animals wandered in the woods until they came to a clearing.

Fragrant wildflowers grew all about the sunny clearing. Little Red Riding Hood stooped to pick them, and in no time had gathered an armload. "What pretty flowers," she said to herself. Then she picked up her basket and made her way back to the path. "I'll have to thank Mr. Wolf for his advice."

The squirrels looked at each other. "Mr. Wolf?" said one of them with alarm. They scurried after the girl.

In the meantime, the wolf had arrived, panting from his long run, at Grandmother's cottage. He waited until he had caught his breath; then he knocked on the door.

"Who is it?" came Grandmother's voice.

"It's Little Red Riding Hood," answered the wolf, mimicking the girl's voice as best as he could.

"The door's unlocked. Come in, my dear," replied Grandmother.

The hungry wolf opened the door and glanced about the room. Then he bounded toward Grandmother's bed, and before she knew what was happening . . .

. . . he had gobbled her up in one bite. The squirrels and mice arrived on the windowsill just in time to see the wolf's misdeed. They looked at each other with alarm. "Little Red Riding Hood will be next on his menu!" exclaimed the squirrel.

"We must get help!" squeaked the mice. The animals raced off into the forest.

The wolf waddled about the cottage. He drew the curtains closed. Then he found one of Grandmother's nightgowns and nightcaps, and slipped these on. He pulled the cap over his big ears, then got into bed and pulled the covers up around his chin.

The wolf was almost asleep, for he was
feeling full, when he heard a knock at the door.
Doing his best to imitate Grandmother's voice,
he called out, "Who is it?"

"It's Little Red Riding Hood," came the girl's voice.
"Come right in, dear," replied the wolf.
Little Red Riding Hood unlatched the door and stepped into the cottage. "My, it's dark in here, Granny," she said. "I've brought you a basket of food from Mother, and some flowers to make you feel better." She tried to sound cheery, but she felt very uneasy. She approached the bed. "Goodness, you don't look at all like yourself," said Little Red Riding Hood. "You must be very sick."

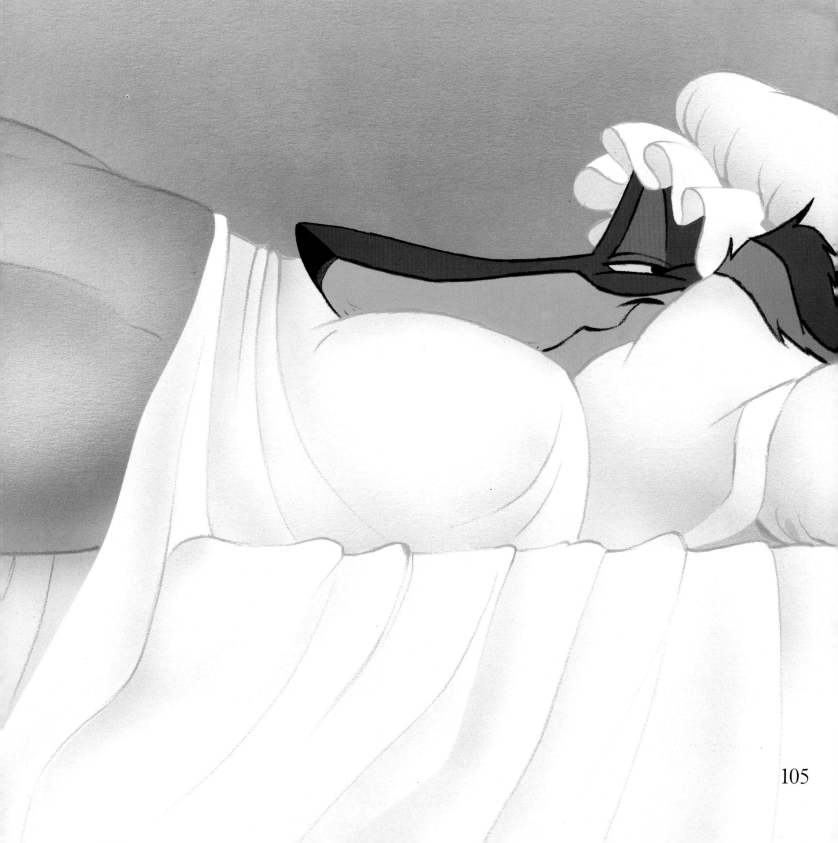

Just then the mice had found a family of
Little Red Riding Hood's rabbit friends in the
woods. "Come quick!" exclaimed the mouse.
"The wolf has eaten Little Red Riding Hood's
grandmother, and next he will eat her! Hurry!
We must save her!"

The mice, squirrels and bunnies scurried
and hopped as fast as they could toward
Grandmother's cottage.

Back at the cottage, Little Red Riding Hood was peering intently at the figure in Grandmother's bed. "My, Grandmother," she said with alarm, "what big eyes you have!"

"All the better to see you with, my dear," croaked the wolf. Just then his ears popped out from under the nightcap.

"Ah, Grandmother. But what big ears you have," said the girl.

"All the better to hear you with," replied the wolf.

"Grandmother! What big teeth you have," she said.

"All the better to eat you with!" cried the wolf, leaping out of bed.

The wolf swallowed Little Red Riding Hood in one gulp. Feeling very full indeed, he walked slowly out of the cottage into the barn. He was looking for a place to take a long nap, and the hay looked inviting. As he nosed about, he felt so pleased with himself that he made up a little song about what a clever wolf he was.

The wolf was so sleepy that he took no notice of the mice and squirrels, chattering in the barn loft. If he had understood what they were saying, he would have taken note of them, for they were busy planning his downfall.

"The pitchfork is ready!" called one of the
squirrels.

"The rope is ready!" called another.

"Patience!" said one of the mice. "Wait until
he's in just the right spot."

The animals held their breath as the wolf
ambled into range, and then . . .

113

. . . *Bonk!* The squirrels let go of the pitchfork handle, and it landed squarely on the wolf's head.

"Bull's-eye!" shouted one of the squirrels. The wolf lay on the ground in a daze.

Quickly, a mouse tied the rope to the wolf's tail. Throwing the rope over a rafter and threading it through a pulley, the animals began hoisting the wolf into the air. It took the strength of every bunny, mouse and squirrel.

When the wolf was fully suspended in the air by his tail, Grandmother and Little Red Riding Hood tumbled out of his open mouth, and landed on the soft hay.

The animals cheered when they saw the two were unharmed, and a bunny explained how they had performed the rescue. Little Red Riding Hood was terribly shaken, but grateful to her animal friends.

"I shall never trust a wolf again," exclaimed the girl. "And when mother tells me to keep to the path, and not speak to strangers, I will do just that!"

Grandmother laughed despite herself, then invited everyone to have some pie. The wolf, in the meantime, had dragged himself up and was slinking into the forest.

The wolf was hungry again, but even worse, he was feeling quite sheepish. Wherever he wandered from that time on, the forest animals remembered his naughty exploit. "Foolish wolf! Foolish wolf!" the birds would call. Then they would titter as the wolf passed by, pretending not to notice. And as for Little Red Riding Hood, she listened more carefully to her mother after her narrow escape, and every morning she scattered bread crumbs and seeds for the animals who had saved her life.

The Emperor's New Clothes

Once, long ago, there lived an emperor who had a great fondness for beautiful clothes. He cared so much about his wardrobe that he had more tailors than soldiers. He attended every social event, and sometimes invented new ones, just to show off his latest fashions. In fact, he had a different outfit for every hour of the day. And he demanded so much flattery that his advisors had little time for anything else.

The emperor's subjects spent half their time attending parades and processions instead of getting their daily work done.

124

But the emperor didn't realize what his vanity was costing the nation. He went right on strutting proudly through the streets in his ever-changing costumes.

The empire's capital city was large and beautiful. Visitors came from far away to see its sights – giving the emperor still more excuses for parades and parties.

His tailors had to work around the clock to keep up with his demands for new finery.

127

The emperor's dressing room was as big as the ballroom of his palace. Every morning, he looked over the rows of magnificent robes, capes, and crowns to choose a wardrobe for the day's events. His servants waited anxiously outside the door for his decisions.

One day, two strangers appeared in the city: a fox named Needle and a monkey, who called himself Thread. They claimed to be master tailors from a faraway country who had come to weave the emperor a set of clothes whose beauty would be unmatched in all the world. In fact, the strangers were swindlers, but news of their coming soon reached the emperor.

When they arrived at the palace, Needle and Thread bowed graciously to the emperor.

"Your majesty," they said, "the marvelous cloth we weave has colors and patterns undreamed of in your realm. Not only that – it has the magical quality of being invisible to anyone who is stupid or unfit for his office."

"How wonderful!" thought the emperor. "Beauty and wisdom combined!"

"Begin your work at once," he ordered.

After receiving a huge sum of money with which to buy materials, Needle and Thread set up their loom and began to pretend they were weaving.

All the fine silver and gold thread they had demanded was hidden away in their room. But the sound of their empty loom was heard in the palace far into the night. Everyone was impressed with their hard work.

135

The emperor was bursting with curiosity about the progress of his new clothes. Finally, he sent his elderly prime minister, Sir Leonine, to see how the work was coming along. Poor Sir Leonine was shocked to find that he couldn't see the cloth displayed so proudly by the weavers! "I must be unfit for my office," he thought humbly. "But I will pretend I can see."

Unwilling to lose the emperor's confidence, Sir Leonine returned to the throne room with a glowing report. "The work is progressing magnificently, Sire. Such patterns! Such colors! It must be seen to be believed."

The emperor was thrilled.

"Spare no expense in supplying the master tailors with everything they require," he ordered. And a steady stream of servants passed into the workroom with bolts of raw silk, spools of glittering metallic thread, and yards of expensive trimming. The two swindlers put all this into their hiding place and continued their pretense of weaving.

Word spread all over the city.
"The master tailors are making the
emperor's new clothes so
magnificent that there will be a
national holiday to see them in a
great procession!"

142

Finally, the emperor could stand
the suspense no longer. He went to
the workroom himself. Imagine his
shock and surprise when he
couldn't see the beautiful cloth
held up before him!

"Great heavens!" he thought. "Am I stupid? Am I unfit to be emperor? How is it that I can't see the cloth?"

But, of course, he pretended to see it. "*Magnifique!*" he cried delightedly.

The emperor was so anxious to conceal his dullness that he called a great assembly and bestowed upon the two imposters the newly created Order of Master Tailor to the Empire!

Once their "weaving" was finished, Needle and Thread pretended to cut the cloth and fit it to a tailor's dummy. The townspeople gathered outside the workroom window to marvel at the beauty of the cloth and the elegant cut of the emperor's new clothes. No one was willing to admit that he couldn't see a thing, lest his neighbors think him stupid.

When the clever swindlers had finished their cutting act, the emperor was called in for fittings. Turning this way and that in his undershirt, he tried in vain to catch even a glimpse of his new clothes. Meanwhile, Needle and Thread kept up a steady stream of admiring chatter as they pretended to measure, tuck, and pin.

At last, the long-awaited day arrived. A special canopy was lifted high above the emperor. The master tailors took their places behind him, pretending to hold up the long trailing train of his rich new robe. Clutching his sceptre nervously, and clad only in his undershirt, the emperor led off the procession.

The townspeople lined the streets in high excitement and cheered when they saw the canopy approaching.

The emperor's subjects applauded loudly and shouted their approval as he paced solemnly along. "What a magnificent robe! And the train! Never has our emperor been so splendidly dressed!"

But suddenly, a small clear voice was heard above the noise of the crowd. "Daddy," said the voice in a tone of wonder, "the emperor has no clothes on." Embarrassed, the father tried to quiet the child. "Don't be silly," he whispered. But the child repeated his words in a louder tone, and the crowd took them up: "The emperor has no clothes on!"

Everyone was so glad that he didn't have to pretend anymore that the whole crowd burst into roars of laughter.

At last, even the emperor burst out laughing! He laughed at his own silliness and the cleverness of Needle and Thread. He laughed at the silliness of his subjects and courtiers, who had been so afraid of looking foolish that they pretended to see what wasn't there. And the master tailors laughed hardest of all – because they had shown that it was more fun to admit you were silly together than to pretend you were wise alone.

160

Puss in Boots

Once upon a time in a village in a kingdom, there lived a miller and his three sons. Now, the miller's family always had enough to eat, but none to spare. One day, the old miller died, and he left his only possessions to his sons. To the oldest son he left his mill, to his middle son he left his donkey, and to his youngest son he left his cat. While the youngest son was fond of the cat, he felt that his father had not dealt fairly, for his brothers could earn a living with a mill and a donkey, but it seemed that little fortune could be made with a cat.

The youngest son was complaining to himself, when suddenly the cat spoke up. "Look here," it said quite plainly. "Get me a fine hat, cape and boots, and I'll see that your future will be bright."

So surprised was the young man to hear the cat speak that he obeyed at once. Taking his last coins, he went into the village and had the clothes especially made. The cat was as pleased as could be when he slipped on the boots, hat and cape. With a wave and a wink, he set off down the road, leaving his master to wonder if he'd been foolish to trust such an eccentric cat.

The cat, who soon came to be called Puss in Boots, wasted no time setting his plan into action. He stepped brightly along the road – stopping now and then only to adjust his hat, or wipe dust from his boots – until he came to a briar patch. There he lay down and pretended to be dead.

Curious at the sight of a cat so richly dressed, and wondering how he might have died there, a rabbit hopped out of the patch. No sooner had the rabbit sat down, when Puss in Boots jumped up and seized it by the ears.

Puss in Boots marched directly to the King's palace, where he boldly insisted on seeing the King at once.

Puss was escorted to the throne room, where he bowed deeply and presented the rabbit, saying, "Greetings, Your Majesty. My noble lord, the Marquis of Carabas, has sent me to deliver this gift to you personally." (The cat had just made up that name for the young man.)

"Please give your master my thanks," said the King graciously. As Puss was leaving, he heard the King asking the Princess if she was ready for their drive along the river.

Puss ran all the way back to his master, and instructed him to go at once to the river to bathe. When the young man questioned him, the cat said, "Trust me. Do as I say, and your future will be bright."

So he did as he was told, and was quite enjoying the water, when he saw the royal carriage approaching. Then he heard Puss shouting, "Help! The Marquis of Carabas is drowning! Help!"

171

When the King heard the familiar name, he ordered that the young man be rescued. "Sire," the cat whispered to the King, so as not to embarrass the Princess, "while my master was bathing, all his clothes were stolen." Puss had cleverly hidden his master's clothes, but the King couldn't know this, so he ordered a servant to fetch one of his finest suits. In no time at all the young man was dressed in a royal outfit that made him look so handsome that, with her father's permission, the Princess asked him to join them in the carriage.

Puss in Boots' job had only begun, however. The clever cat rushed down the road ahead of the carriage, until he came to a large field that the peasants were reaping. "Listen here!" he shouted. The peasants stopped to listen. "The royal carriage will be here shortly. When the King asks who owns these fields, you must tell him they are owned by the Marquis of Carabas, or you will be severely punished."

The peasants nodded agreement, afraid even to speak. "Now back to work with you!" ordered Puss.

Soon the royal party arrived, and the King ordered the carriage to stop. "Who owns these fields?" he called to the peasants.

Glancing nervously at the cat, the peasants replied, "The Marquis of Carabas owns all these fields, as far as you can see!"

"Ah!" said the King, leaning back in his seat. "And fine fields they are, young man."

The miller's son nodded and smiled, not knowing quite what to say. But the Princess took his silence for modesty, and was growing fonder of him by the minute.

The young man glanced out the window to see if Puss in Boots might give him some clue as to the nature of his plan, but the cat had already hurried away. Puss ran ahead of the carriage until he came to an enormous castle. The castle was owned by a dreaded ogre, who also owned all the fields along the road. The cat trotted across the drawbridge.

Upon his request, Puss in Boots was escorted to the ogre's chamber.

"Pardon me," said the cat, removing his hat with a flourish. "I had to make your acquaintance, having heard tell of your fame far and wide."

The ogre was flattered, but replied gruffly, "I've no time for vanities. What is it you want?"

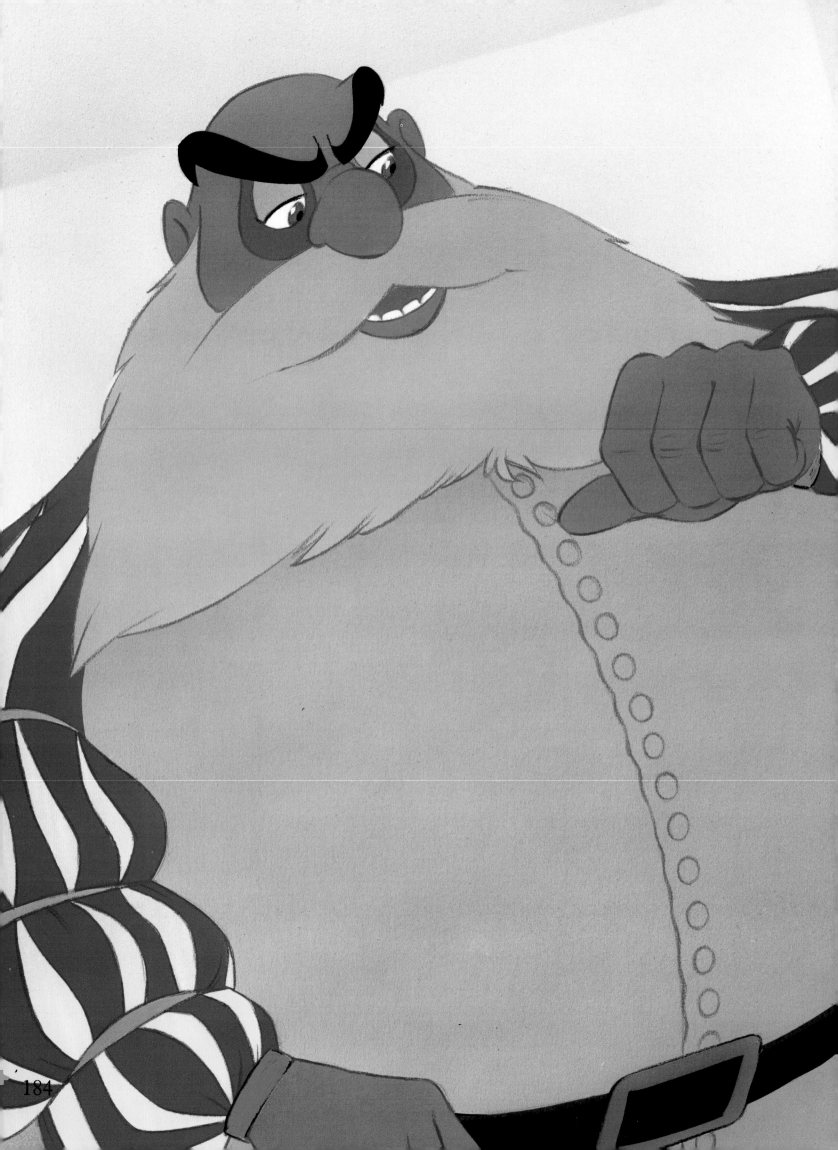

"I have no doubt you are as fierce and brave as folks say," spoke Puss in Boots. "But I cannot believe the stories that you can transform yourself into anything you want."

"I shall prove I can do just that!" thundered the ogre. "And then you shall die as a reward for doubting one so great as I."

185

Before Puss in Boots could say another word, the ogre turned himself into a ferocious lion. The ogre's words dissolved into angry roars, and as he waved his huge paw in the air, the cat couldn't help noticing how large and sharp his claws were.

Puss was frightened nearly out of his boots, but quickly regained his composure. "If you please!" he shouted, to be heard above the roars. "That *is* as amazing a feat as I've ever seen. But I should think it quite impossible to change yourself into something as small as, say, a mouse." No sooner had he spoken the words, then the vain ogre turned himself into a tiny fieldmouse.

"Splendid!" cried Puss, clapping his paws together.

"And now I shall eat you!" cried the cat. As quick as a wink, Puss in Boots caught the mouse and ate him in one bite. Then he put on his hat, cleaned his whiskers, and made his way about the castle, sternly informing all the servants that they were soon to meet their new master.

Soon the royal carriage arrived, for the castle stood at the end of the road. Puss in Boots greeted the royal party at the gate. "Welcome to the castle of the Marquis of Carabas!" he exclaimed. "Perhaps you'd like some refreshment after your journey."

The King was delighted that his new friend, whom his daughter appeared to be very fond of, lived in such a splendid castle.

"My house is your house," said the young man with a humble bow.

The group went into the Great Hall, where a cold banquet had been quickly prepared by order of the cat. The King proposed that the Marquis marry his daughter, and when the happy couple agreed, they lifted their glasses in a merry toast.

197

A lavish wedding was planned for the Marquis and the Princess, who were so obviously in love. No one in the kingdom could doubt that it was a joyous event, for on the day of the wedding, all the bells in the land rang out the good tidings. Lords and peasants alike were invited to the wedding, in which Puss in Boots played a part by proudly holding the Princess' train.

No one was more surprised at the wedding than the groom's brothers, to whom the new Prince promised land and wealth. When the brothers asked how he had come to his fortune, he winked and replied, "I'll explain later."

As for Puss in Boots, after three days of wedding festivities, he thought he should be very happy to spend the rest of his days chasing mice and pretending that he was just an ordinary cat..

Goldilocks
and the
Three Bears

On a summer day not so very long ago, a little girl played with her three teddy bears in the shade of a big tree. The girl, who was called Goldilocks, on account of her shiny golden hair, had spent the whole morning in the woods. She and her teddy bear friends had discovered a turtle, several toads, a ladybug, and many patches of pretty flowers. Then they began to feel sleepy and sat down to rest.

"You know," said Goldilocks with a yawn, "I really like those toads we met, and the turtle was awfully cute, but I want to meet some big animals. Maybe a bobcat, or a deer, or some real bears would be nice . . ." But Goldilocks didn't finish her sentence, because the warm breeze and chirping birds had lulled her to sleep.

Suddenly, Goldilocks heard her mother calling. And because she
was a rather naughty girl, and she didn't want to go home, she
jumped to her feet and ran deeper into the woods. She clutched her
teddy bears as she ran, and though they were cross at being bumped
around so, and worried about getting lost, they kept silent.

Before long Goldilocks came to a delightful little house that she had never seen before. Flowers bloomed in window boxes, and there were three doors of different sizes. "I wonder who lives here!" exclaimed Goldilocks.

Goldilocks knocked on the littlest door, but there was no answer. Then she opened the door and went inside. "How adorable!" said Goldilocks.

The house was neat as a pin, and a delicious smell was in the air. Then Goldilocks saw a wooden table with three bowls of porridge on it. Suddenly, she felt quite hungry. She dipped a spoon into the largest bowl, but found the porridge much too hot. Then she tried the middle-sized bowl, but it was too cold.

"This is just right!" she exclaimed, sampling porridge from the littlest bowl. And she ate it all up. Her teddy bears sat on the table. They also felt hungry, but were much too polite to eat someone else's food without permission.

"What shall we do next?" asked Goldilocks, gathering up her teddy bears. She peered into the living room and saw three chairs of different sizes. She tossed her teddy bears into the largest chair, and climbed up beside them. "This chair is much too big," she said, dangling her feet over the edge.

Then Goldilocks noticed a middle-sized chair. "Let's try that one," she said to her teddy bears, and they all got into it. "It's not quite right either," she said. Then Goldilocks saw a little chair by the table, and when she sat in it, she found it was just the right size.

She leaned back in the chair
and put her feet up on the
table, even though she knew it
was a naughty thing to do.
Suddenly, the chair legs
screeched out from under her,
and Goldilocks fell over
backward. She was not hurt,
but the chair broke into several
pieces.

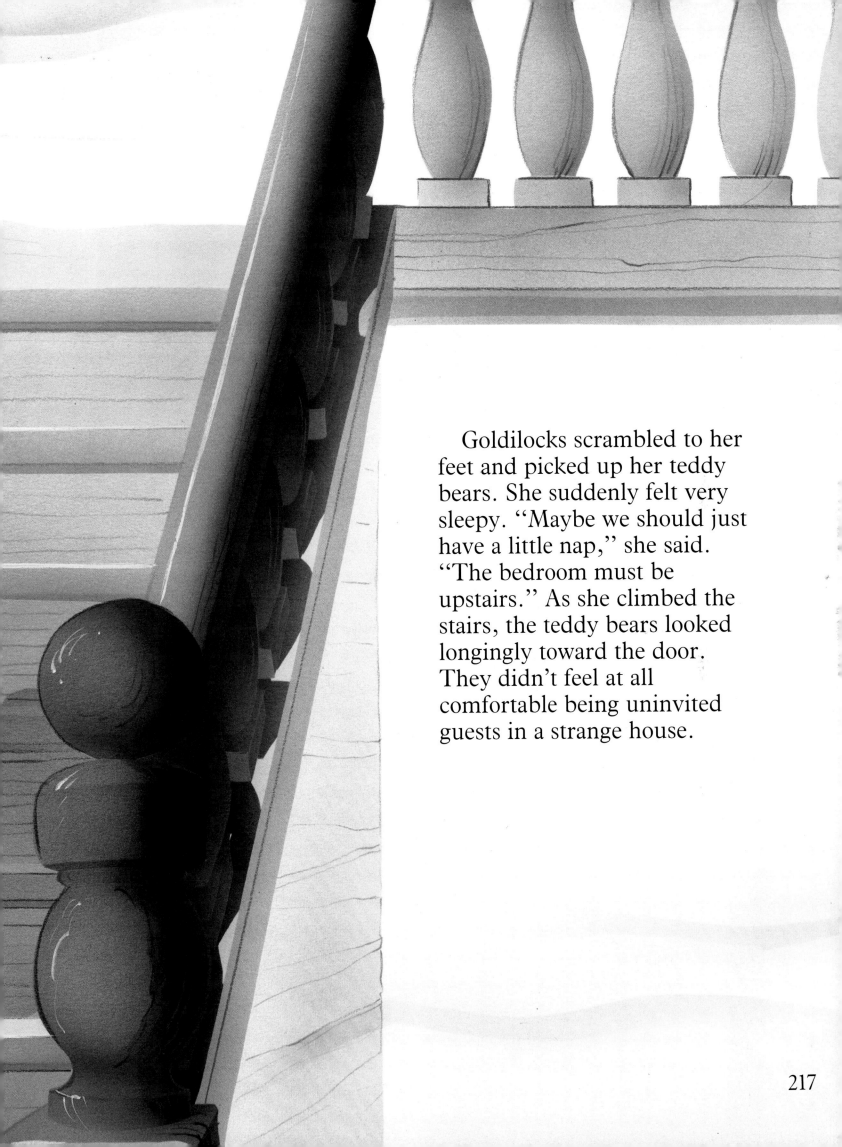

Goldilocks scrambled to her feet and picked up her teddy bears. She suddenly felt very sleepy. "Maybe we should just have a little nap," she said. "The bedroom must be upstairs." As she climbed the stairs, the teddy bears looked longingly toward the door. They didn't feel at all comfortable being uninvited guests in a strange house.

With a little push from Goldilocks' elbow, the bedroom door swung open. There before her were three beds of different sizes. "Look at that!" exclaimed the girl. "Perfect for an afternoon nap."

She ambled down the row of beds. "Let's play house!" she said to her teddy bears. "I'll be the mommy, and you'll be my three little children. You've just brushed your teeth, and now you're ready for bed."

With that, Goldilocks tucked the teddy bears into the smallest bed. "Now I'll sing you a lullabye," she said. She sang so sweetly, and the bed was so comfortable, that the teddy bears soon forgot their worries. They would have drifted off to sleep, but suddenly Goldilocks had another idea.

"Let's have a slumber party!" she exclaimed, pulling the teddy bears out of bed. "We'll tell secrets and have pillow fights and eat popcorn . . . if we had some."

Goldilocks scrambled onto the largest bed, but it seemed much too hard, even for telling stories. Then she tried the middle-sized bed, but it felt too soft and lumpy. So she flopped onto the smallest bed, and began telling the teddy bears made-up secrets.

In the meantime, the three bears who lived in the house were returning from their midmorning walk. "The porridge must be cool by now," shouted Baby Bear, "and I'm hungry!" He ran ahead as Papa Bear tried to hurry up Mama Bear, who was gathering wildflowers along the way.

But when the bear family approached their house, they knew something was wrong. Mama Bear remembered having closed the door carefully when they went out, yet now the door was ajar. "I'm going to get to the bottom of this," said Papa Bear gruffly. The three bears went quietly inside.

"Oh no!" cried Baby Bear.

"Someone's made a mess of our table," said Papa Bear sternly. "And they've tasted my porridge," he added, glancing into his bowl.

"Someone's been eating my porridge, too," said Mama Bear.

"Someone's been eating my porridge," exclaimed Baby Bear, "and it's all gone!" Sadly, he held his bowl upside down.

"Look!" said Papa Bear. "Someone's been sitting in my chair!"
And Mama Bear said, "Someone's been sitting in *my* chair!"
And Baby Bear wailed, "Somebody's been sitting in my chair, and it's all broken to pieces!"

Then Baby Bear had an idea. He rushed to the stairs. "Maybe they're upstairs!" he cried. "Let's catch them!"

"Be careful, son," cautioned Papa Bear. "Wait for us."

The three bears climbed the creaky stairs and opened the bedroom door. "Someone's been sleeping in my bed!" growled Papa Bear.

Mama Bear frowned. "Someone's been sleeping in my bed, too," she said.

Then Baby Bear squealed, "Someone's been sleeping in my bed, and they're all still here!"

The bears' anger at their messy intruder vanished when they saw the sleeping Goldilocks, who looked very innocent. She was curled in Baby Bear's bed with her teddy bears, who were doing their best not to act alarmed. Baby Bear tugged on his mother's skirt and pointed to the girl. "Can we keep her?" he asked. But when Mama Bear scowled back at him, he didn't ask again.

Goldilocks awoke with a start, frightened to see the bears gathered at her bedside. She jumped off the bed and rushed out the door, down the stairs, and out of the house.

She was in such a hurry that she even forgot her teddy bears. Mama Bear, Papa Bear, and Baby Bear rushed after her, shouting things like, "Wait! We won't harm you!" and "Come back and make us fresh porridge!" But Goldilocks' only thought was to get away.

"What a close call!" she thought, as she ran through the woods. "Mother would be so angry with me if she knew . . ." And suddenly she could hear her mother calling.

Goldilocks sat up and stretched. "Coming, Mother!" she called. Then she looked at her teddy bears. "What a strange dream I had," she said. "But that's all right. You're here!" And the teddy bears wondered what they had done to deserve the big hug she gave them.